WE BOTH READ

Parent's Introduction

We Both Read books are specially designed to invite parents and children to share the reading of a story by taking turns reading aloud. This "shared reading" innovation, which was developed with reading education specialists, invites parents to read the left-hand pages. Children can then be encouraged to read the right-hand pages, which feature words and text specifically written for their level of ability. With books at five different reading levels, the *We Both Read* series is perfect for pre-readers, as well as beginning and reluctant readers!

Reading aloud is one of the most important activities parents can share with their child to assist them in their reading development. However, *We Both Read* books go beyond reading **to** a child and allow parents to share the reading **with** a child. As you read together, you will find the *We Both Read* books igniting interest in reading and accelerating reading development!

You may find it helpful to read the entire book aloud yourself the first time, then invite your child to participate in the second reading. We also encourage you to share and interact with your child as you read the book together.

If your child is having difficulty, you might want to mention a few things to help them. "Sounding out" is good, but it will not work with all words. They can pick up clues about the words they are reading from the story, the context of the sentence, or even the pictures. Some stories have rhyming patterns that might help. For beginning readers, you also might want to suggest touching the words with their finger as they read, so they can better connect the voice sound and the printed word.

Sharing the *We Both Read* books together will engage you and your child in an interactive adventure in reading! It is a fun and easy way to encourage and help your child to read—and a wonderful way to start them off on a lifetime of reading enjoyment!

Parent's Page ➡  ⬅ Child's Page

Take turns reading!

We Both Read: My Day

Picture Book Edition

Reading Level (Child's Pages) – Pre-K to K

Text Copyright ©2007, 2002 by Sindy McKay
Illustrations Copyright ©2007, 2002 by Meredith Johnson
All rights reserved.

We Both Read® is a trademark of Treasure Bay, Inc.

Published by Treasure Bay, Inc.
40 Sir Francis Drake Boulevard
San Anselmo, CA 94960 USA

Printed in Malaysia

Library of Congress Catalog Card Number: 2006937429

ISBN-10: 1-60115-005-9
ISBN-13: 978-1-60115-005-9

We Both Read® Books
Patent No. 5,957,693

Visit us online at:
www.webothread.com

WE BOTH READ ®

My Day

By Sindy McKay

Illustrated by Meredith Johnson

TREASURE BAY

 I hear my clock ringing. My day has begun.

My day always starts with my good friend the . . .

. . . sun.

My mom says, "It's time to get up, sleepy head!
It's time to get up and get out of your . . .

. . . bed."

I rush to get dressed. I know just what to choose!
I find both my socks. Then I look for my . . .

. . . shoes.

It's time to wash up—make the dirt disappear!

I take extra care when I clean out my . . .

. . . ear.

I run down the hall with my doggie named Tom.
We rush to the kitchen and both hug . . .

. . . my mom.

My mom gives me toast with the butter-side up.
She gives me some juice in my favorite blue . . .

 . . . cup.

Old Tom likes toast, too. (He's a bit of a hog.)
But Mom gives him food that is made for . . .

. . . a dog.

My mom says to hurry—there's no time to fuss!

I race down the sidewalk and hop on . . .

. . . the bus.

We head off for school—we don't want to be late!

Our teacher is waiting for us by the . . .

. . . gate.

She leads us inside and we sit on a rug.

She reads us a story about a . . .

. . . big bug.

We draw and we cut and we use lots of glue.

And when we use crayons, I always choose . . .

 . . . blue.

At lunch I sit next to my friend Patrick Napes.

He loves to eat apples, but I prefer . . .

. . . grapes.

It's back to the classroom to learn this and that.

We learn about numbers and how to spell . . .

Cat

 . . . cat.

The final bell rings. It's too loud to ignore!

I leap from my desk and I rush out . . .

 . . . the door.

The bus picks me up. We drive right by a lake!

At home Mom is waiting with milk and some . . .

. . . cake.

I watch some TV and I play for a tad.

I hear a car coming! I know it's . . .

. . . my dad.

We're hungry for dinner. We help as we're able.

My dad carries food out, and I set the . . .

. . . table.

It's time for my bath. Here I go! Rub-a-dub!

Dad turns on the water and fills up . . .

. . . the tub.

The sun has gone down now. Mom peeks in to look.

I hop into bed and we open . . .

. . . a book.

Mom tucks me in tight and I'll be asleep soon.

My day always ends with my good friend . . .

. . . the moon.

If you liked *My Day,* here is another *We Both Read* picture book you are sure to enjoy!

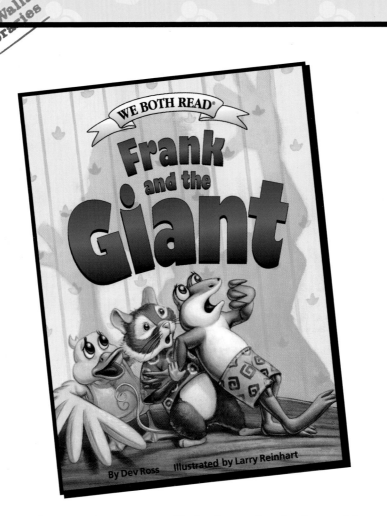

Frank, an adventurous little frog, is playing with his friends, when suddenly his ball flies off and bounces into the house of a giant! Frank's friends are too scared to help him get his ball back, so he sneaks into the huge house all by himself. There, he is discovered by the giant, who seems big and scary to Frank, but who is really a friendly little boy.

To see all the *We Both Read* books that are available, including over 35 titles available in paperback, just go online to **www.webothread.com**